W9-DCU-207

Dunc and Amos
and the
Red Tattoos

OTHER YEARLING BOOKS YOU WILL ENJOY:

THE COOKCAMP, *Gary Paulsen*
THE VOYAGE OF THE *FROG, Gary Paulsen*
THE BOY WHO OWNED THE SCHOOL, *Gary Paulsen*
HOW TO EAT FRIED WORMS, *Thomas Rockwell*
HOW TO FIGHT A GIRL, *Thomas Rockwell*
HOW TO GET FABULOUSLY RICH, *Thomas Rockwell*
CHOCOLATE FEVER, *Robert Kimmel Smith*
BOBBY BASEBALL, *Robert Kimmel Smith*
IT'S A WEIRD, WEIRD SCHOOL, *Stephen Mooser*
THE HITCHHIKING VAMPIRE, *Stephen Mooser*

YEARLING BOOKS/YOUNG YEARLINGS/YEARLING CLASSICS are designed especially to entertain and enlighten young people. Patricia Reilly Giff, consultant to this series, received her bachelor's degree from Marymount College and a master's degree in history from St. John's University. She holds a Professional Diploma in Reading and a Doctorate of Humane Letters from Hofstra University. She was a teacher and reading consultant for many years, and is the author of numerous books for young readers.

For a complete listing of all Yearling titles,
write to Dell Readers Service,
P.O. Box 1045, South Holland, IL 60473.

Gary Paulsen

Dunc and Amos and the Red Tattoos

A YEARLING BOOK

Published by
Dell Publishing
a division of
Bantam Doubleday Dell Publishing Group, Inc.
1540 Broadway
New York, New York 10036

If you purchased this book without a cover you should be aware that this book is stolen property. It was reported as "unsold and destroyed" to the publisher and neither the author nor the publisher has received any payment for this "stripped book."

Copyright © 1993 by Gary Paulsen

All rights reserved. No part of this book may be reproduced or transmitted in any form or by any means, electronic or mechanical, including photocopying, recording, or by any information storage and retrieval system, without the written permission of the Publisher, except where permitted by law.

The trademark Yearling® is registered in the U.S. Patent and Trademark Office.

The trademark Dell® is registered in the U.S. Patent and Trademark Office.

ISBN: 0-440-40790-7

Printed in the United States of America

May 1993

10 9 8 7 6 5 4 3 2 1

OPM

Dunc and Amos and the Red Tattoos

Chapter · 1

Duncan—Dunc—Culpepper sat on the edge of his bed checking off items on the list he was holding. His best friend Amos Binder called them out to him.

"Swim trunks."

"Check."

"Mosquito repellent."

"Check."

"Sleeping bag."

"Check."

"Fake throw-up."

"Ch—hey, that's not on the list."

Amos grinned. "You never know. Just when

you leave something at home, that's the very thing you'll need."

"This camp we're going to has some pretty strict rules about behavior. Willie Myers told me that Attila the Hun doesn't have anything on these counselors."

Amos took off his cap and put it on backward. "How come we got so lucky? Whose brilliant idea was it to send us off to Camp Gitchee Goomee, anyway? What a name. Have we done something to deserve this kind of punishment?"

Dunc looked at him.

"I mean lately," Amos said.

"My mother says that everyone should have the experience of going to summer camp. She thinks it will be good for me to get back to nature, breathe some fresh air, and be around normal people my age."

"What am I—abnormal?"

"Oh, I'm sure she didn't mean anything against you, Amos. Besides, you're coming with me."

"I've been thinking about that. This camp business sounds worse than the army. I could stay here and hold down the fort until you get back. Lie around the pool, soak up some rays, play some video games."

"Amos Binder, I can't believe it. We always do everything together. I can't believe you would even think of such a thing!"

"I was going to write to you."

Dunc decided it was time to try a different approach.

"Okay, Amos. If that's the way you want it. I can handle that. No problem here. *She* might be a little disappointed, though."

"She?"

"Melissa Hansen. I found out that she just happens to be going to the same camp we are."

Dunc knew it wasn't fair to bring up Melissa. Amos loved Melissa with his whole heart. While she thought of him as a welcome mat—if at all.

Amos put his cap on the right way. "Do you know for sure, guaranteed, beyond a shadow of a doubt, cross your heart and hope to eat raw liver, that Melissa is going to this same camp?"

"Where do you think my mother got the name of the camp?" Dunc nodded. "Melissa's mother told her."

Amos jumped from the floor up to the bed. "Ye-es! All alone with Melissa Hansen in a beautiful mountain setting. Birds singing, flowers blooming . . ."

"I hate to mention this, Amos, but you won't be all alone with her. There will be at least two hundred other campers, besides the counselors. They put the boys on one side and the girls on the other."

"Details," Amos said, ignoring Dunc. "What an opportunity! It'll really be the perfect place to show off my skills as an outdoorsman."

"I didn't know you had any."

"I've got three days. I'll get some."

Dunc smiled. "Well, if you're determined to go on this trip, who am I to stand in your way?"

Chapter·2

Camp Gitchee Goomee was nestled in a small mountain range near Silver Lake. All of the buildings were made log-cabin style. There were twenty bunk houses, ten on each side of the camp. The dining hall, recreation room, office, and infirmary were located in the middle.

"Isn't this something? I told you it would be great up here, Amos. Just breathe in some of that fresh air."

"I'd like to, but breathing is not one of the things I do best right now."

Amos looked like a giant raccoon. He had a small piece of white tape across his nose, and his eyes were two perfectly round black circles.

"Tell me again how you managed to break your nose."

"It happened last night. I was bringing my camping gear downstairs when the phone rang. I figured it was Melissa calling to talk about camp stuff. It sounded like her—you know, that kind of high-pitched ring."

Dunc nodded. Amos was always certain that Melissa was calling him. She didn't give him any reason to think it might be her. She had never called him. In fact, she had never even acknowledged his existence on this planet. Or any other planet.

"Anyway, as you know, I like to get it by that all-important second ring. So she doesn't have to wait. I slid the rest of the way downstairs on the banister. I cut off a lot of time right there. You should have seen me. I was really cooking."

"Is that when it happened?"

"No, not yet. I was looking good. I ran wide open down that short hall to the kitchen, rounded the turn, and then my mother opened the pantry closet door. I hit it face-first, full blast."

"How much damage did you do?"

"It knocked me out cold for two hours and left an imprint of my face in the door. Forever. It's worked out okay, though. My mom's going to have it framed and use it as a portrait. Save some money."

"That's really tough. I mean about your nose. Maybe camping will take your mind off it."

Several busloads of campers had been steadily arriving. Each camper was assigned a cabin, a camp team, and a counselor.

Dunc read their names off a list on the bulletin board. "We are the Blue Jays, in cabin seven. I'm bunk eighty-eight, and you're eighty-nine."

"At least they put us together," Amos said. "I don't know if I could handle all this fresh air with strangers."

They lugged their suitcases and sleeping bags across the exercise yard to cabin seven. Inside the cabin were two rows of metal army cots, a door marked OFFICE, and another marked LATRINE.

"It's not home, but it'll do." Amos yawned. "I'm beat." He stretched out on his cot.

A piercing whistle filled the cabin.

Amos flipped out of the cot and landed face-down on the cold cement.

"Camper eighty-nine. No lying on the cots except during a designated sleeping time. That will be one demerit."

Amos shook himself, tried to straighten his nose, and looked up. A mountain, posing as a man, was walking toward him, holding a silver whistle and carrying a clipboard.

"Camper eight-nine, you obviously have not read the Gitchee Goomee Campers Handbook. It lists all the camp regulations and the punishment for each infraction. See to it that you read it immediately."

Amos dragged himself up off the floor.

The mountain folded his arms and glared. "I am Counselor Adolf. I am assigned to this cabin. You are answerable to me for each infraction of camp rules." He turned and marched back to his office.

"Is that guy for real?" Amos whispered. "Did you see the size of his arm? He makes the Terminator look like a sissy."

Dunc watched Adolf until he was out of sight, then shook his head. "He probably eats cats. Kittens." Dunc looked at his watch. "I think we'd better get over to the dining hall before we miss dinner."

"Duncan."

Dunc knew Amos was serious when he used his full name instead of his nickname.

"Did you know about this? Did you know we'd get demerits for breathing and have a storm trooper for a counselor?"

"You always get way too excited over things, Amos. He's probably a real nice guy—once you get to know him."

"I don't want to get to know him. I'd rather get to know a grizzly bear. Are you holding anything else back from me?"

"Nothing comes to mind, Amos." Dunc looked out the window. "I did tell you it was strict here, remember?"

"Strict is one thing. Prison camp is another."

"Things will look up after you eat," Dunc said. "By the way, did I tell you that we eat at the same time the girls do?"

He knew it would work.

Amos smoothed down his hair and headed for the door. "Well, come on. What are you waiting for?"

Chapter · 3

Amos was excited. "I think I see her. At least, I think it's her. See the one with her back to us in the third row from the left?"

Dunc started to answer when a man at the head table stood up and blew his whistle.

"These guys have a thing about whistles, don't they?" Amos said.

The man was short and about as wide as he was tall. He had white hair, chubby cheeks, and could have passed for Santa Claus. Except for the shorts.

"Attention, campers!" He tapped his knife on the table until everyone quieted down. "Attention! I am your camp director, Mr. Wiggleston. I would like to take this time to personally welcome each and every one of you to Camp Gitchee Goomee. Before you are dismissed this evening, I have a few short announcements."

Mr. Wiggleston took a deep breath, and the middle button popped off his shirt.

"First, we must all take note of the posted schedules. This is how we know we are in the right place at the right time. If you have kitchen duty, be sure to show up five minutes early for your assignment. Remember our camp motto—A busy camper is a happy camper."

Amos put his head down on the table. "We have KP? You didn't tell me we had to wash dishes!"

Dunc put his finger to his lips. "Shh. The man is trying to talk."

"Some of you new campers may not have heard about our end-of-camp party."

A loud squeal came from the girls' side.

Mr. Wiggleston cleared his throat. "It is a camp tradition to use the money made at the concession stand from the previous year's camp, to host the next camp's farewell party."

Another loud squeal.

"However, a word of warning. In order to attend the party, you can have no more than ten demerits . . ."

"As fast as they hand out demerits around here, they won't have to worry about having a party," Amos whispered.

". . . so work hard, play hard, and enjoy your stay here at Camp Gitchee Goomee. Now, except for those of you with kitchen duty, you are dismissed."

"I feel sorry for the poor guys who have kitchen duty tonight," Amos said. "Look at this mess."

Dunc looked down at the floor. "I don't know how to tell you this. . . ."

Amos stared at him. "Oh, man! Are you serious? You mean we have KP the *first* night?"

"Look at it this way, Amos. After tonight, we've got a full week until it's our turn again."

"I can't wait."

The kitchen was full of boys from cabin seven. The leader seemed to be a short, chunky kid who had been to camp before.

"Hiya. I'm Toby Gillis. Your job assignment

13

is on that wall over there. When you find it, I can tell you the fastest way to get it over with."

Amos read the assignment. "Garbage. We're garbage."

Toby laughed. "Everyone has their problems."

He showed them how to tie off the sacks and where to take them. "Be sure you put the lids on tight, so the animals can't get to it."

There were ten sacks in all. The garbage cans were located down a little hill inside a fence. The sacks were stuffed as full as possible, and they were heavy. Between them, Dunc and Amos could carry only one at a time.

"At least we didn't have to wash dishes," Dunc said.

Amos tried to get a better grip on his end of the sack. "No. We got the much classier job of hauling everyone's gross, smelly leftovers a half-mile to the garbage cans. We can hardly see where we're going."

"It could be worse."

Suddenly the end Amos was holding burst under the pressure. Food and trash exploded all over him.

Green stuff dripped down his face. Pieces of tomato and other, unidentifiable, vegetables clung to his ears, nose, and clothing.

Amos wiped some of the slime off with his sleeve. "Would this qualify as worse?"

Dunc just shook his head.

It took longer to pick up the loose garbage than it did to carry all the rest of the sacks down the hill.

Amos fell to his knees. "I'm tired. This is the last one. Let's sit down a minute."

"We can't. It's getting late." Dunc tried to pull him up. "Somebody might wonder what's taking so long. We better get back—wait, someone's coming. Duck behind the cans."

Footsteps walked up to the trash cans. There was the sound of a lid opening and something being dropped in.

"Too dangerous to try it tonight," a deep voice whispered. "We'll have to wait for the right time. Don't worry. When it does happen, it'll be the end of Wiggleston this time."

The footsteps walked off into the dark.

"Did you hear that, Amos? Something's going on here. Those guys want to get rid of Wig-

15

gleston. Too bad we didn't get a look at them. Hmmm."

"Stop it," Amos said.

"What?"

"You know, that *hmmm* sound and that la-la-land stare. Every time you get that look, I wind up doing things I'm sorry for. Like that time I wore your sister's clothes."

"Amos, aren't you curious? Don't you want to know what those guys are up to?"

"I don't care. And you shouldn't, either. The only thing we should be worried about is trying to survive the next two weeks."

Dunc lifted one of the trash-can lids. "Look at this. Our suspect left a gum wrapper."

"Will you stop it? We don't have a suspect. Unless gum chewing is illegal."

Dunc walked back toward the kitchen, mumbling to himself, and Amos followed, his shoulders drooping. "Something tells me I'm in for it."

Chapter · 4

Amos was dreaming. A large sack of garbage was chasing him all over the dining hall, blowing a silver whistle.

"Get up, Amos! We're going to be late for the flag ceremony."

Amos opened one eye and then the other. "What time is it?"

Dunc looked at his watch. "It's five-fifteen. Adolf blew the wake-up whistle at five o'clock. Everybody else is already outside. Hurry."

"Hurry? At five o'clock in the morning? Are you kidding? It's still dark outside." Amos turned over. "Wake me when it's time for breakfast."

17

"Come on, Amos." Dunc shook him. "Breakfast is right after the flag ceremony."

Amos covered his head with a pillow. "Then call me in time for lunch."

Dunc looked out the window. "Oh, no! Adolf is coming this way. It's going to be demerit city. Get *up!*"

Amos crawled out of his sleeping bag. He was completely dressed, including shoes and socks.

Dunc stared at him. "Weren't you a little uncomfortable?"

"I thought it might save time. And I was right."

They hustled out the back door before Adolf came in the front and made their way to the mess hall.

Breakfast was blue powdered eggs, raw hash browns, and watery orange juice.

"Yum," Amos said. "No wonder this place has its own doctor. I bet most of his patients are food-poisoning victims."

Dunc was pushing the blue eggs around the plate with his fork. "What do you suppose those guys last night have against Wiggleston?"

"Probably nothing. You know how it is. Sometimes you say things. You don't exactly expect people to hide behind garbage cans and listen."

"This is different. I can feel it. I've been checking around. All the counselors here are new, except Adolf and a guy named Chuck. The only other men in camp are Mr. Phillips, who has been the caretaker here for years, Dr. Stevens, and Mr. Wiggleston."

"So?" Amos shrugged.

"So the guy we heard last night is someone with something against Wiggleston. It would have to be someone who's been here awhile."

"Why don't you wait until you have a crime before you try to solve it? That's the way it usually works," Amos said.

Mr. Wiggleston blew his whistle and stood up to make an announcement. His face was red, and he was obviously upset.

"Campers, I have some most distressing news. It has just been reported to me that the money—the concession stand money and the equipment fund, several hundred dollars—is missing from the vault. If anyone has any information about this, please report to my cabin at once."

"Bingo!" Dunc said. "The crime. Now all we have to do is put it together."

"What's with this 'we' stuff? Wiggleston said to report any clues to him. Let's not get involved in this one. Okay?"

"But I have a plan."

"How did I know you were going to say that?" Amos sighed. "You always have a plan. But listen to me just this once. We aren't—"

"We already know which of the men are possible suspects. We need to find out if any of the women could be in on it," Dunc said.

"If this plan involves me and girls' clothes, I'm out of here." Amos turned to leave.

"I think Melissa would be our best bet, don't you?"

Amos spun around. "You know, that Mr. Wiggleston seems like a pretty nice guy. I'd hate to stand by and see him get in trouble or maybe fired when we could have done something about it."

Chapter · 5

"Melissa didn't recognize me. She never even got a good look at my face."

Amos was standing in front of the mirror in the bathroom examining his bruised chin.

"She didn't recognize you because you spent the whole time lying facedown on the porch in front of her cabin," Dunc said.

"Can I help it if that board was loose? I only missed that next step by a fraction of an inch."

"You didn't miss it, Amos. You caught it. With your chin."

Amos rubbed his chin. "At least you got your information. None of the women are involved.

They're all new this year. All I got was a bruised chin. I didn't even get to talk to her."

"Cheer up, Amos. I know for a fact you had her attention. She'll probably ask around about you now."

Amos started out the door. "Do you think so? We could walk back by her cabin so she could get a good look at my face this time."

Dunc grabbed his sleeve. "Maybe later. We've got work to do. Besides, you've got two whole weeks left to impress her."

"Don't remind me. Two weeks of this place. I don't know if I can take it. Mosquitoes the size of F-15s. Food I'd be embarrassed to feed to my dog Scruff. Exercising. Marching. Whistles in your ear. And those are the good points."

Dunc was studying a list of names. "Okay, these are our suspects. Two counselors, Adolf and Chuck. The doctor and the caretaker. We're looking for two of them with something against Mr. Wiggleston."

Amos looked at his watch. "I'd love to stay and help you out, but it's time for our bird-watching class." He made a circle in the air with his finger. "Yippee. Today we are looking for the ruby-throated hummingbird."

"This is great, Amos! Just the break we needed." Dunc nearly ran over him, heading for the door.

Amos watched him leave. "I never knew you liked bird-watching."

Mr. Ramos, the bird-watching instructor, spent forty-five minutes describing the bird's personality. Then he assigned each team a pair of binoculars and an area to watch.

Dunc charged up a small hill and quickly sat down behind some oak brush. He was looking intently through binoculars.

Amos was out of breath from trying to keep up. "I . . . never . . . knew that . . . you . . . were . . . so interested in birds."

"Sit down, Amos. You're blocking my view of the infirmary."

"What makes you think a ruby-throated hummingbird will land on the infirmary?"

"Amos. Help me watch our suspects. This is a great opportunity. From up here, we can watch all of them at the same time."

"Oh. Suspects. I knew that. Really. I knew that."

After about thirty minutes, Dunc stood up to stretch his legs. "So far all we've seen is Mr. Phillips raking leaves and the two counselors, Chuck and Adolf, working with kids. We're not going to get anywhere at this rate."

"This could be something." Amos pointed toward the infirmary. "Adolf is talking to the doctor. Now they're going into the infirmary."

Dunc grabbed the binoculars just in time to see the two men go through the doorway.

"This could be it. We've got to get inside that infirmary."

Amos laughed. "You're not the only one who wants in. It's the only way to get any rest in this place."

A look came over Dunc's face.

"What does that look mean?" Amos started backing away.

Dunc smiled. "I think I just thought of a way to get inside. . . ."

Chapter · 6

"This will never work. It isn't logical. This guy's a doctor. He knows when people are sick. They teach you that stuff in doctor school."

"Trust me, Amos. This will work. Besides, you're not supposed to be sick sick. Just a little sick. Come on."

Amos walked slowly down the hill. "Why do I have to be the sick one? Why can't I be the concerned friend?"

Dunc turned and put both hands on Amos's shoulders. "I can't be the sick one because I look too healthy. You know, pink cheeks, good color. You, on the other hand, are pale, thin, and kind of yellow, and your face looks like it was hit by a train."

"Yellow? I'm yellow? I look that bad?" Amos put his hand to his forehead. "Come to think of it, I haven't felt so hot lately. I think I've got a fever. Maybe I do need a doctor."

Dunc tried to hide a smile. "Come with me, Amos. I'm sure he can fix you right up."

They stopped at the door in front of the infirmary.

Dunc whispered, "Now, don't forget. You stay sick until I get a chance to look everything in here over for clues."

By this time, Amos was holding one hand on his forehead and the other on his stomach. "I don't see that as a problem."

Dunc opened the door and poked his head in. Dr. Stevens and Adolf were shaking hands. Adolf took a step back when he saw the boys and growled at them.

"What are you two doing here? You should be with your activity leader. Failure to stay with your activity leader is five demerits!"

Dunc quickly pulled Amos inside the office.

"My friend here doesn't feel well. Could you take a look at him, Doctor?"

Adolf headed toward the door. "We'll discuss this later."

Dr. Stevens was a small, thin man. He wore a white coat, and his round wire glasses kept sliding down his long nose.

"Help your friend up onto the table. I'll just wash my hands."

Amos started moaning. Kind of a low, sick animal moan.

"Don't overact," Dunc whispered.

"Who's acting?"

The infirmary was a small building. The examining station was on one side, and the other side was used to store medical supplies. Small white boxes with red markings were stacked halfway to the ceiling.

Dunc began to look around the room. There was a license to practice medicine hanging on the wall. A large oak desk sat in the corner with papers piled on it.

"I don't feel so good, Doc. I think it was something I ate." Amos moaned.

Dr. Stevens shook the thermometer. "It usually is."

While the doctor was busy examining Amos, Dunc edged around to the desk. The paper on top of the pile said something about a delivery date in Mexico. Dunc frowned, thinking, I wonder what a doctor from here would be delivering all the way to Mexico?

"Hey!"

A loud voice startled him. He jumped back and landed on the doctor's black patent-leather shoes.

"My desk is off limits, son. Come over here to the waiting area and have a seat." The doctor pointed at a chair.

"Do you know what's wrong with him, Doctor? Is it serious?" Dunc eased into the chair.

The doctor studied Dunc's face a few moments before answering. "Your friend doesn't have a temperature. I can't really find anything wrong with him."

He handed Amos a slip of paper. "Take this to your cabin counselor. It gives you permission to lie down until you feel better."

Amos sat up and smiled weakly. "Thanks, Doc. I'll let you know if I make it."

Outside the door Dunc said, "Wait here. I need to check on something."

Amos leaned against the building for support. "Deserted in my hour of need."

Dunc crawled under the window and inched up so that he could see inside. "Aha! Just what I thought."

"What? What's going on?"

Dunc crawled away from the window. "Dr. Stevens is hiding the evidence. I saw some kind of shipping order for Mexico on his desk. He must have been worried about it. He practically ran to the desk and stuffed it into his pocket."

"Is that all? Here I am on my deathbed, and all you can do is talk about Mexico and evidence. Can't you see I need to get some rest?"

"Amos, stop that! You're not sick. We made it up. Remember?"

"I ought to know if I'm sick or not. And I'm sick. Help me make it to the cabin."

"Okay, okay. Lean on me. I'll take you to the cabin. But you're not really sick—it's just *psychosomatic*."

"I knew it probably had a big name. If I don't live through the night, I leave all my personal belongings to you. Take extra good care of my goldfish."

Dunc started to explain that *psychosomatic* was a word, not a disease. That Amos's sickness was all in his head. But he changed his mind. Instead, he led Amos up the hill to the cabin and tucked him in.

Chapter · 7

"Has he left yet?" Dunc whispered.

"Not yet."

"Keep watching."

They were lying flat on their stomachs under the caretaker's small cabin. Dunc was watching the back steps while Amos kept an eye on the front.

"I'm not so sure I should be under here," Amos said. "I might get sick again."

"You'll be fine. Trust me."

"You keep saying that. And I keep winding up doing weird things."

Dunc turned and looked at Amos. "We're here because we have to narrow down our list of suspects. The only time Mr. Phillips is sure to be gone is during mealtime. As soon as he leaves we'll take a look around. Simple."

"So simple, I'm getting cramps in my elbows."

"Every good detective has to learn to deal with adversity."

"And that's another thing. Stop using words that are bigger than you are." Amos scooted back. "There he goes! Amazing. I can't believe anybody would hurry to eat in this place. This guy is actually running."

They inched out from under the back of the cabin. Dunc brushed the dirt off his clothes. "We'll do it just as we planned. You keep watch, and I'll take a look around."

The inside of the cabin made World War II look good. Clothes were thrown everywhere. Trash was all over the floor. It was hard to walk across the room without stepping on something.

Amos closed the door behind them. "Ugh! Something smells like it had a bad time in here."

"Get over to the window and watch. We don't want to get caught."

"Now he thinks of this."

"Amos."

"I'm watching. I'm watching."

Dunc picked up one piece of trash after another. "This is going to be harder than I thought. This guy is a pig."

Amos glanced out the window. "Uh-oh. He's coming back. Quick—hide."

Dunc dived under the bed without seeing where Amos went.

The front door opened. Mr. Phillips walked to his dresser and put something in a drawer. He looked in the mirror. Picked at his teeth. Then he turned and went back out the front door.

Dunc crawled out from under the bed. "All clear. You can come out now."

"Amos?"

"Amos? Where are you?"

A muffled noise came from the closet.

"Humm-mee."

"Amos, are you in there?" Dunc jerked open the closet door.

"Help me."

Amos was sticking headfirst in a narrow, dirty clothes hamper. His feet were waving wildly in the air.

"How did you manage? . . . Never mind. I'll have you out in a minute."

He pushed on the hamper until it tipped over. Then he held on while Amos crawled out backward.

Amos peeled some dirty clothes off his head. "At least I know where that awful smell is coming from." He pointed at the hamper. "Year-old socks. Gross."

"I think we may be getting somewhere, Amos. I saw Mr. Phillips put something in the dresser."

Dunc pulled open the drawer. Inside was an ink pad and stamp. It was in the shape of a strange red flower.

"Great," Amos said. "I get gassed by socks that can stand on their own, for a stamp that makes a red flower."

"That's not all. Look at this."

Under the ink stamp was a photograph of

some guys in army uniform standing in front of a bunch of tents. Dunc took it out.

They were all there: the doctor, Phillips, Adolf, and Chuck.

"What does it mean?" Amos asked.

"I don't know. But we sure are going to find out."

Chapter · 8

It was raining. The exercise field could have been used for a mud bog rally. All the boys were moved inside the dining hall for arts and crafts.

"What *is* this thing?" Amos held up a tangle of blue, red, and yellow plastic strings.

"It's supposed to be a key chain. Kind of a souvenir," Dunc said.

"These guys are sick. Who would want a souvenir of this place? Two minutes after I leave here, this place is forgotten, never to be thought of again or even mentioned under penalty of death."

Dunc was busy writing on a small pad of paper. "Maybe you could give it to your mother."

"Yeah, right. 'Here, Mom. Thanks for spending all that money to send me to camp. I brought you a deformed key chain.'"

Amos quit trying to weave the plastic strings. "What are you writing?"

"I'm trying to make some sense out of the clues we've found. Here's what we have so far: a gum wrapper, a threat, a suspicious handshake, something being shipped to Mexico, an ink stamp of a red flower, and a picture."

Dunc looked up. "It doesn't make any sense."

"I'm glad we finally agree on something."

"Seriously, Amos. We've got one week—"

"And counting the minutes."

Dunc made a face. "As I was saying. We've got one week left to put all of this together. I've heard rumors. If that money isn't found, Wiggleston is going to be fired."

Chuck walked over to their table. He resembled a large baboon. His bottom lip stuck out two inches farther than his top, and his arms swung as he walked.

"You worms get to work. No slackers. Hup hup, keep it up, two three four."

He walked on to the next table.

Amos picked up his plastic strings. "Marine Corps. Definitely."

Dunc stared at Chuck. "Did you see that?"

"How could I miss him? He makes the Empire State Building look like a tollbooth."

"No. His arm. Look at his right arm. A tattoo."

"Lots of ex-servicemen have tattoos. So?"

"In the shape of a red flower?" Dunc smiled. "Amos, something is going on here. I think they're all in on it: the doctor, the caretaker, Adolf, and Chuck. Somehow we've got to figure out what it is."

Amos had woven his finger into the middle of his key chain. It was stuck. "Why don't you just go ask him?"

Dunc's face brightened. "That's what I like about you, Amos. You're always one step ahead of everybody else."

Amos shook the key chain. He tried pulling it off. It wouldn't budge.

Dunc reached over and pulled some of the plastic strings loose. "Like I was saying. You always know just the right move."

Amos jerked his finger out. "What are you talking about?"

"I was just saying how amazing you are. Brilliant, actually."

Amos cocked his head to one side. "Okay. Let me in on it. What is it that you *think* you're going to talk me into?"

Dunc smiled. Kind of a cat-that-swallowed-the-canary smile.

Amos waited.

"Great idea. Asking him. But you need to hurry. Arts and crafts won't last much longer."

"Hey. I didn't—I mean, I don't . . . I was only—"

Dunc pushed him toward the front of the room. "Try not to be too obvious. Just tell him you noticed his tattoo. Ask him where he got it and what it stands for."

Chuck was standing with his arms folded, glaring at everything.

Amos gulped. "Ah. Chuck?"

"What do you want, kid? Make it quick."

"I, ah, was just noticing your arm there, and I just wondered if you lifted weights or something."

Amos had hit on the one thing Chuck loved to talk about. He started flexing his muscles and making them wiggle. He went through a whole routine before Amos could stop him.

Amos looked back at Dunc and shrugged.

"Ask him," Dunc mouthed.

Amos waited patiently until Chuck finished his routine. "That's great. You being able to do that. I can honestly say I've never seen anything quite like it."

Chuck grinned. "Wanna see it again?"

"No. That is—I noticed you have a tattoo."

"So. What's it to you?"

"I was just wondering where you got it."

Chuck made the flower look like it was dancing on his arm. "I got this baby during the war."

"Does it mean anything in particular?"

Chuck's voice changed into a snarl. "None of your business, maggot head! Go sit down."

Amos started backing away. "Gee, thanks, Chuck. It's been real nice talking to you."

He turned and moved back to the table.

"What did you find out?" Dunc asked.

"About muscles—it's disgusting. He wiggles them. About tattoos—zero. He's not talking."

Chapter · 9

It was two o'clock in the morning. Twenty-four boys had gathered near the lake and were smearing mud on their faces.

"I shouldn't have told you I'd do this," Dunc said.

Amos grinned. Not a little grin—his face was covered with mud, and all you could see were teeth. "That's usually my line. It sounds funny coming from you."

Dunc slung a wad of mud off into the darkness. "I just don't understand why we have to do this. It seems kind of mean."

"Toby Gillis says that all first-year campers

have to pull a raid on the girls' cabins. If they don't, they're marked men for the rest of camp."

"What's so bad about being marked?"

"He says they do stuff to you. Like fill your sleeping bag with spiders and snakes. Sometimes they wait until you're in the shower and hide all your clothes. One guy stayed locked in the latrine for three days until a counselor found him." Amos shivered.

"Do you think they'd do that kind of stuff to us?"

Amos nodded. "In a heartbeat."

Dunc hesitated. "I can see where that might be a problem. But I really need to concentrate on the case. We don't have much time."

"Come on," Amos pleaded. "I'll help you work on the case tomorrow. I'll even go along with any dumb ideas you come up with. I just don't want to wake up next to a snake."

"Okay. I said I'd go. But it still seems kind of mean."

"Toby says the girls really like it. He says they look forward to it every year."

The group had their instructions: Spread

out. Do your job. And most of all, don't get caught.

They moved like a silent army across the exercise field. Dunc, Amos, and a boy named Rubio had been assigned the outside of cabin eight. Two others had the inside.

In six minutes, while the girls slept, the inside was turned into a complete disaster. String was tied cobweb style from cot to cot. The doorknobs were loosened to fall off at a touch. The latrine stalls were all locked from the inside, and dirt and honey were poured on the floor in strategic places.

The outside was almost finished. Toilet paper hung from every available place. All of the windows except one had been soaped.

"Hurry up, Amos! Everybody's leaving," Dunc whispered.

"I'm trying to. But I can't get this window to close. Get something for me to stand on."

Dunc looked around. "There isn't anything. Leave it. Come on."

"I've almost got it. Come over here, and give me a boost."

Dunc cupped his hands and lifted Amos up.

He was about to shut the window—when he saw her.

Melissa.

There she was. Second cot from the end. The most beautiful girl on earth sleeping like an angel.

He leaned inside the window and let out a long, deep sigh.

By this time, Dunc was weaving under the strain. "What are you doing up there, Amos? I can't hold you much longer!"

Amos pulled himself up to the window ledge and sat on it.

"Are you crazy?" Dunc hissed. "Get down here!"

Amos was like a lovesick puppy. He sat in a trance and would have probably sat that way the rest of the night except that he lost his balance.

He dropped through the window like four pounds of rotten yogurt in a three-pound bag and landed face-first in a pile of dirt and honey. His eyes were glued shut. His mouth was full of dirt. He rolled around on the floor fighting the string cobwebs until he was covered from head

46

to toe with honey and dirt and completely tangled in the string.

He finally got to his feet and started for the door, but he tripped on the string and fell flat on one of the cots.

That was when things started to go bad.

"Swamp monster! Help!" somebody screamed.

Amos was going around in circles, waving his arms trying to keep his balance. He still couldn't see, and the only sound he could make was a low growl.

The girls' counselor tried to get out of her office, but the doorknob was hanging halfway off and she couldn't open the door.

By this time every girl in the cabin was jumping on her cot screaming.

"Get it out of here! Somebody save us!"

Dunc pulled himself up to the window to see what was going on.

A few of the girls had started throwing things at Amos: shoes, hairbrushes, pillows, footlockers, bunks.

Dunc shook his head. This had to be Amos's all-time worst. For a second he thought about leaving Amos behind. No—they'd probably hang him from the flagpole when this was all over.

Dunc sighed and slid through the window. Maybe nobody would recognize him with mud on his face, he thought.

"It's me," Dunc whispered as he took Amos by the hand. "Step over the string when I tell you."

The girls continued throwing things as Dunc and Amos disappeared out the door into the night.

Chapter · 10

"You really don't look that bad—considering," Dunc said.

"Considering what? That I'm not in traction?"

Amos was missing patches of skin on his arms. His face had strange purplish bruises, and he had a few bald spots on his head from rubbing too hard to get the goo out.

Dunc picked up his notepad. "It's not as bad as it could have been. For one thing, we didn't get caught."

Amos tried to mash some of his hair over to cover one of the bald spots. "I wonder if Melissa knows it was me."

"No, she doesn't. And you're not going to tell her. Ever."

"She probably knows."

"Get real, Amos. You had every girl in that place ready to kill you. They all thought you were the Monster from the Black Lagoon."

Amos sighed. "It would be like her to pretend she didn't know—to protect me."

Dunc decided to ignore him. Otherwise, Amos might talk about Melissa for the rest of the year. He was trying to come up with the ultimate plan, one that would put his whole case together and solve it at the same time.

"Do you remember that promise you made last night?" Dunc asked.

Amos looked up. "Promise?"

"You said that if I went on the raid with you, you'd go along with any plan I came up with."

"I think my exact words were 'any *dumb* ideas' you came up with. You're not going to hold me to it after all that's happened, are you?"

A tiny smile started at the corner of Dunc's mouth.

"After all," Amos went on, "I was under a lot of pressure last night. People were threatening me. My life was in danger. Who knows what horrible—"

"You did promise," Dunc interrupted.

Amos knew he was stuck. "Okay. But just how far off the wall is this next great idea of yours?"

Dunc took his arm. "It's not all that bad. Come on, I'll tell you more about it on our way."

"On our way to where?"

"We've got almost an hour before our next activity. I figure that ought to be just about enough time."

Amos stopped walking. "Enough time for what?" His voice started to get loud. "How am I supposed to know what my part is in this demented plan, if you don't tell me the plan?"

"Shh." Dunc pulled him off the path and looked around to make sure no one was listening.

"Here's the deal. I need to get back inside the doctor's office. This time we need to take a good look. The only way to do that is if the doctor is somewhere else."

Amos shrugged. "So?"

"I need you to get him out of his office."

"And just how am I supposed to do that? He eats and sleeps in that place. He wouldn't leave if it were on fire."

"I thought about fire. Too close to the trees. I figure the only sure way to get that doctor out of his office is to tell him somebody is sick or maybe dying."

"I still don't get it," Amos said. "Who's sick?"

Dunc was starting to get frustrated. "Nobody is sick! You just knock on the door. Tell him somebody up in the woods is hurt and needs a doctor real bad. He'll take off, and we'll search his office. Easy."

"What if he doesn't fall for it?"

"It's your job to make absolutely sure he does. Now come on. We've wasted too much time already."

Amos moved to the front of the infirmary. He raised his hand to knock on the door.

Suddenly the door burst open. The doctor rushed by him carrying his medical bag, trying to put on his white coat at the same time.

He looked surprised when he saw Amos. "Unless it's an emergency, son, I can't help you

52

right now. Somebody fell on the hiking trail. They may have a broken leg."

The doctor ran across the exercise field and up toward the woods. Amos stood there with his mouth open and his hand raised.

Dunc came out from the side of the building. "I'm impressed, Amos. You must have told him something good to make him run like that."

Amos watched the retreating doctor. "You know you can always count on me."

The inside of the infirmary looked the same as before.

"You search his sleeping quarters. I'm going to have a look at that desk again," Dunc said.

After about ten minutes, Dunc called out, "Have you found anything yet?"

Amos walked back into the room. "I found that same army picture with all of them in it. Nothing else, though. How about you?"

Dunc shook his head. "He's moved everything that was on the desk. But I know there's something here. We're just missing it somehow."

They looked around the walls of the infirmary. Nothing seemed out of place. Amos took a step backward and knocked down a stack of the white medical boxes.

Dunc picked up one of the boxes. "Amos, you've got to be more careful—wait a minute, look at this!"

The top of the box had been stamped with an exotic red flower.

"Let's open one," Amos said. "It's probably drugs or something illegal."

Dunc opened a box. "Medical supplies." He opened several others. "They all have medical supplies."

Amos scratched his head. "I don't get it. Why would anybody go to the trouble of putting that red stamp on a bunch of medical supplies?"

Dunc was deep in thought. He snapped his fingers. "It all fits together. Amos, we've got to get the sheriff up here."

Chapter · 11

"It's time. Everybody's over in the dining hall now. Do you know what to do?" Dunc asked.

Amos was sitting at a desk in front of the camp's intercom system. "I know what to do. You've made me go over it five thousand times."

They had waited until everyone from the administration office had gone to lunch and just walked right in the front door. Dunc used the phone to call the sheriff. Amos was about to use the intercom.

Dunc started for the door.

"Give me five minutes."

He ran as hard as he could to the dining hall and positioned himself behind a tree.

Amos watched the clock. The seconds ticked by. He took a deep breath and flipped the switch. A loud crackling noise came over the system.

He cleared his throat. "Attention, all campers! May I have your attention please!"

Amos grinned. Part of him wanted to do what Dunc said, but another part was starting to get into it. The microphone was too much.

"All you boys and girls out there in Gitchee Goomee-land. This is your lucky day. I'm comin' at you with an announcement that is guaranteed to blow your socks off."

From behind his tree Dunc could hear the intercom clearly. He frowned—what was Amos doing? Man, if he messed this up . . .

By now, Amos had the microphone in one hand and was whirling around the room, talking like a disc jockey on a radio.

"Be glad you tuned in today, kiddies. We have a way-out news flash just for you. The stolen money has been found. I repeat—the concession stand and equipment fund money has been found."

Dunc had his eyes on the door of the dining hall. He could still hear Amos.

"Stay tuned to this station for further events. Reported straight to you as they happen. But now let's get down. Back to the music. Our request line is open twenty-four hours a day. We play the hottest tunes. Completely uninterrupted by commercials."

Amos looked at his watch. Five minutes exactly. Sadly he put the microphone down and raced out the door.

Dunc was starting to wonder if their plan was going to work.

He needn't have worried.

The front doors of the dining hall flew open. Chuck, Adolf, and Mr. Phillips came barreling out. Dunc followed at a distance.

They ran past the bushes where Amos was waiting. He fell in behind Dunc.

The men ran to the infirmary and burst in, leaving the door open.

Dunc moved to one side of the door, put his fingers to his lips, and motioned Amos to listen at the other side of the door.

Mr. Phillips yelled into the doctor's face.

"What was that all about? How could anyone have found it? You were supposed to have hidden it!"

Chuck stuffed about five pieces of gum into his mouth. "Yeah, Major. You said it was hid real good."

The doctor pulled a key out of his pocket and unlocked the medicine cabinet. He moved some of the items and felt around on the bottom shelf. He pulled out a blue zippered pouch and opened it.

"It's all here safe and sound. That intercom stunt must have been a joke. Just some punk kids playing around. Don't worry." He put the pouch back in the medicine cabinet.

Dunc smiled—he and Amos had them. Everything was going exactly the way he had planned.

Or it was until Amos hiccuped.

Amos clapped his hand over his mouth, but it was too late. Everyone in the room turned and looked in their direction.

The boys turned to jump off the porch, but Adolf and Chuck grabbed them in midair and held them up like dead fish.

"What have we here?" The doctor looked at them over the top of his glasses. "You two have been here before. Perhaps once too often."

The two counselors threw them into the middle of the floor in a pile.

Dunc rubbed his sore throat. "Excuse me, gentlemen. We were trying to locate the rest room. Could any of you direct us?"

Chuck grabbed him by the front of his shirt. "Shut up, dog breath! You speak only when the major speaks to you. Got it?"

Dunc nodded.

Mr. Phillips was nervous. He kept chewing the same fingernail and repeating, "What are we going to do?"

"Get ahold of yourself, Theo," the doctor ordered.

He looked at Adolf. "Sergeant, close the door and pull those curtains shut."

The doctor was clearly in charge. He put his hand on Dunc's shoulder.

"We have an unfortunate situation here. But not one that can't be easily remedied."

He patted Amos's head. "These children will simply have to be held until it's safe."

Amos looked at Dunc.

The doctor went on. "Our operation is far too cost-effective to let a little problem like this get in our way." He jerked his thumb toward the side room. "Lock them in there for now."

Chapter · 12

Amos sat down on the bed. "I don't guess our getting caught figures into your overall plan."

Dunc was listening at the door. "Not so you could tell it."

"The sheriff *did* say he was coming, didn't he?"

"I don't know how seriously he took my call. He said he'd send a unit as soon as one became available."

Amos started to worry. "What if that's not until next month?"

The conversation from the other room started to get loud. The doctor was trying to convince the rest of them to ship the medical supplies tonight, then just tell everybody the boys were making it all up.

"Our contacts in Mexico will pay double if we can pull this off tonight."

"What's he talking about?" Amos whispered.

Dunc frowned. "Somehow these guys are using this camp as a base for stolen medical supplies. Their symbol is that red flower. They ship the stuff to somewhere in Mexico. Wiggleston must have gotten suspicious, so they tried to get him out of the way."

Amos put his head in his hands. "What are they going to do to us?"

Dunc rubbed his chin. "Let's try not to think about that right now. Help me find a way out of here."

He looked around the room. There were no windows because it was an add-on to the original cabin. The only door was the one they had come through. A rock fireplace took up one whole corner. The only furniture in the room was a bed and a dresser.

Dunc moved over to the fireplace. "Help me move this screen."

Amos looked at him. "I really don't think this is the time to redecorate."

"Get over here."

"Okay, okay."

They moved it to the side. Dunc bent down and looked up the chimney.

"You're not going to do what I think you're going to do, are you?" Amos asked.

Dunc crawled inside the fireplace. "I think one of us might be able to squeeze through here."

"One of us?"

"The top gets a little narrow."

"One of us?"

"Amos, you're our only hope. You may be thin enough to get through. I'd get stuck for sure."

Amos shook his head. "Things always happen to me."

"Hurry, Amos. I think they're through talking. You've got to go. Now."

Amos crawled into the fireplace. The inside rocks gave him footholds and helped him work his way up.

He was almost out when the door burst

open. Adolf grabbed Dunc's arm. "Where's the other one?"

"What other one?"

"Don't get smart with me, kid! Where's your friend?"

"Dunc!" Amos screamed. "I'm stuck up here! I can't move!"

Adolf reached up into the fireplace. He grabbed Amos's foot and pulled his tennis shoe off. "Come out of there, you little runt!"

Amos was wedged in tight. He could just see over the top of the chimney. He saw Mr. Wiggleston walking across the exercise field with a deputy sheriff.

"Over here!" Amos yelled. "Help!"

Chapter · 13

They were home. Amos was stretched out on the bed watching Dunc unpack.

"I still can't believe we pulled it off," Dunc said. "That gang of crooks has been into black marketing since their days in the war together. It kind of gives you a good feeling to know they're behind bars."

Amos arranged the pillows. "Right now, there are only two things that give me a good feeling. One is being able to lie on this bed. Just because I want to. The second is not being stuck in that stupid chimney."

"That was bad. Especially when that forest

ranger grabbed your legs to pull you down. You should have had your belt tighter."

"I don't want to talk about it."

"Those pants came right off."

"I said I don't want to talk about it."

"It wouldn't have been so awful, except they finally ended up pulling you out from the top."

"I *really* don't want to talk about it."

"Who would have guessed that the whole camp would turn out to watch?"

"Dunc!"

"I can understand how you feel. If a couple hundred people saw me covered with soot, running around on a roof in my underwear, I might be a little upset too."

"Are you through?"

"I'm only trying to sympathize with you. Tell you what a bad deal I thought it was."

Amos sat up. "You've told me. Now, if we never talk about that dumb camp again, it will be too soon."

"I just need to tell you one more thing."

"Only one?"

Dunc held up his hand. "I promise."

"Okay. But only one."

"We got a letter from Mr. Wiggleston."

"That's nice."

"He was so grateful to us that he sent us a reward."

"Really? How much?"

"It's not money."

Amos started to lie back down. "Well, if it's not money, what is it?"

"He gave us five free summers at camp."

Downstairs the front door slammed and Dunc turned around.

Amos was gone.

Be sure to join Dunc and Amos in these other Culpepper Adventures:

The Case of the Dirty Bird

When Dunc Culpepper and his best friend, Amos, first see the parrot in a pet store, they're not impressed—it's smelly, scruffy, and missing half its feathers. They're only slightly impressed when they learn that the parrot speaks four languages, has outlived ten of its owners, and is probably 150 years old. But when the bird starts mouthing off about buried treasure, Dunc and Amos get pretty excited—let the amateur sleuthing begin!

Dunc's Doll

Dunc and his accident-prone friend Amos are up to their old sleuthing habits once again. This time they're after a band of doll thieves! When a doll that once belonged to Charles Dickens's daughter is stolen from an exhibition at the local mall, the two boys put on their detective gear and do some serious snooping. Will a vicious watchdog keep them from retrieving the valuable missing doll?

Culpepper's Cannon

Dunc and Amos are researching the Civil War cannon that stands in the town square when they find a note inside telling them about a time portal. Entering it through the dressing room of La Petite, a women's clothing store, the boys find themselves in downtown Chatham on March 8, 1862—the day before the historic clash between the *Monitor* and the *Merrimac*. But the Confederate soldiers they meet mistake them for Yankee spies. Will they make it back to the future in one piece?

Dunc Gets Tweaked

Dunc and Amos meet up with a new buddy named Lash when they enter the radical world of skateboard competition. When somebody "cops"—steals—Lash's prototype skateboard, the boys are determined to get it back. After all, Lash is about to shoot for a totally rad world's record! Along the way they learn a major lesson: *Never* kiss a monkey!

Dunc's Halloween

Dunc and Amos are planning the best route to get the most candy on Halloween. But their plans change when Amos is slightly bitten by a were-wolf. He begins scratching himself and chasing UPS trucks: He's become a werepuppy!

Dunc Breaks the Record

Dunc and Amos have a small problem when they try hang gliding—they crash in the wilderness. Luckily, Amos has read a book about a boy who survived in the wilderness for fifty-four days. Too bad Amos doesn't have a hatchet. Things go from bad to worse when a wild man holds the boys captive. Can anything save them now?

Dunc and the Flaming Ghost

Dunc's not afraid of ghosts, although Amos is sure that the old Rambridge house is haunted by the ghost of Blackbeard the Pirate. Then the best friends meet Eddie, a meek man who claims to be impersonating Blackbeard's ghost in order to live in the house in peace. But if that's true, why are flames shooting from his mouth?

Amos Gets Famous

Deciphering a code they find in a library book, Dunc and Amos stumble onto a burglary ring. The burglars' next target is the home of Melissa, the girl of Amos's dreams (who doesn't even know that he's alive). Amos longs to be a hero to Melissa, so nothing will stop him from solving this case—not even a mind-boggling collision with a jock, a chimpanzee, and a toilet.

Dunc and Amos Hit the Big Top

In order to impress Melissa, Amos decides to perform on the trapeze at the visiting circus. Look out below! But before Dunc can talk him out of his plan, the two stumble across a mystery behind the scenes at the circus. Now Amos is in double trouble. What's really going on under the big top?

Dunc's Dump

Camouflaged as piles of rotting trash, Dunc and Amos are sneaking around the town dump. Dunc wants to find out who is polluting the garbage at the dump with hazardous and toxic waste. Amos just wants to impress Melissa. Can either of them succeed?

Dunc and the Scam Artists

Dunc and Amos are at it again. Some older residents of their town have been bilked by con artists, and the two boys want to look into these crimes. They meet elderly Betsy Dell, whose nastly nephew Frank gives the boys the creeps. Then they notice some soft dirt in Ms. Dell's shed, and a shovel. Does Frank have something horrible in store for Dunc and Amos?